FAIRY TALES

A Classic Collection

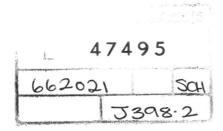

First published in Great Britain in 2004 by Zero To Ten Limited
2A Portman Mansions, Chiltern Street, London W1U 6NR

This edition © 2004 Zero To Ten Ltd
© LAROUSSE/VUEF 2002
© LAROUSSE/S.E.J.E.R 2004

British Library Cataloguing in Publication Data:
A CIP catalogue record for this book is available from the British Library

ISBN 1-84234 280 0

FAIRY TALES
A Classic Collection

ZERO TO TEN

CONTENTS

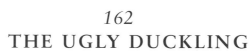

SNOW WHITE

Once upon a time, deep in the snowy midwinter, a queen sat sewing at her window. As she watched the slow, heavy snowflakes fall, she pricked her finger with her needle. Three fat drops of blood fell onto the snow, where their startling redness caught the queen's eye.

"If only I could have a child with skin as white as that snow, lips as red as that blood and hair as dark as this ebony window frame."

And later she did have a child, a daughter, with skin as white as snow, lips as red as blood and hair the colour of ebony, so they named her Little Snow White. But the joy of the birth was overtaken by sorrow, for as soon as the child was born the queen died.

A year later the king married again. His new wife was beautiful, but also very jealous. She hated the thought that anyone might look lovelier than she. She had a magic mirror, which she kept secret from everyone. Every so often she would look in the mirror and say:

"Mirror, mirror, on the wall,
Who is the fairest of them all?"

And the mirror would answer:

"Why you, my queen, are the fairest of all."

And this pleased the queen, for she knew the mirror spoke only the truth.

But Snow White grew more beautiful with each passing day. Soon she was as bright as the light of day itself and more lovely than the queen.

So, when the queen asked the mirror:
"Mirror, mirror on the wall,
Who is the fairest of them all?"

The mirror replied:
"You, my queen, are beautiful it's true,
but Snow White is much fairer than you."

The queen was furious and turned green with envy. From that moment whenever the queen looked at Snow White she felt sick with jealousy and hatred. The queen's envy grew worse every day, until there was no room in her body for any other feelings.

When the queen could take no more she summoned a huntsman.

"Take Snow White into the forest and kill her. I want proof you have done it, so bring me back her heart."

With a heavy heart, the huntsman took Snow White into the forest. Just as he was about to stab her with his hunting knife, Snow White burst into tears.

"Dear huntsman," she said, "please let me live and I will run away into the forest and never return."

The huntsman was only too happy to grant her wish as he loved Snow White as much as anyone else.

At that moment a young boar came running by. He killed it and cut out its heart to give to the queen as proof of Snow White's death. The queen was overjoyed when she saw it for she now believed that she was the fairest in the land again.

Although Snow White was not dead, she was all alone in the dark and frightening forest. She jumped at every noise and tripped over every root. As she had no idea what to do she ran in one direction and didn't stop until the evening. Just as it was turning dark she spotted a small cottage. She knocked at the door, but no one answered. She tried the door and it swung open. Desperate for somewhere to rest, Snow White went in.

Inside the tidy little house was a table with seven little plates laden with food and seven small mugs. And against one wall were seven little beds, all neatly made.

Snow White was so hungry that she took a bit of food from each plate and a sip of drink from each mug. Then, realising just how tired she was she tried the beds. Finding one which suited her, she stretched out and fell asleep.

The sun had set when the owners of the house returned. They were seven dwarves who mined for gold in the mountains. It wasn't long before they realised that

everything in the house was not
how they left it.

"Someone's been sitting in my chair," said one.

"Who's been fiddling with my plate," said the second.

"My bread's been nibbled at," said the third.

"My vegetables have gone," said the fourth.

"My fork's been used," said the fifth.

"And my knife," said the sixth.

"And someone," spluttered the seventh, "has been drinking from my mug!"

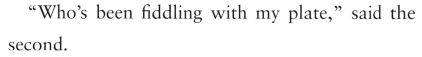

Then the first dwarf noticed that his bed was a bit messy. "Someone's been lying on my bed!" he exclaimed.

"Mine, too!" said the others.

It was the seventh dwarf who found Snow White sleeping in his bed. He called the other dwarves over and they all stared at their unexpected visitor. Snow White was blissfully unaware of the disturbance she was causing, and slept on in the deep sleep of the innocent.

"My word," said the dwarves, "she is beautiful. We'll let her sleep and find out who she is in the morning."

When Snow White woke, she had a huge shock at being surrounded by seven curious dwarves. But their easy smiles and kind nature comforted her and she was soon answering their eager questions. She told them all about her wicked stepmother and how she had tried to have her killed. And she told of how the kind huntsman had let her go and how she had run all day until she came upon the dwarves' house. The dwarves were entranced by her tale. "If you can take care of the house for us," they said, "then you can stay here for as long as you like."

"Oh yes!" cried Snow White. "That sounds perfect."

So every day, when the dwarves left for the mountains, Snow White tidied the house; and every evening when the dwarves returned, Snow White made them all dinner.

However, during the day Snow White was all alone. The dwarves warned her to take care. "Your stepmother will realise sooner or later that you are still alive. She'll come looking for you, so do not let anyone in."

Sadly, the dwarves were right. One day the queen stood before her magic mirror again, for the first time in a long while.

"Mirror, mirror, on the wall,

Who is the fairest of them all?"

And the mirror replied,

"You, my queen, are beautiful it's true, but Snow White who lives with the dwarves in the mountains is fairer than you."

The queen was furious! She knew the mirror did not lie, so it meant the huntsman had not killed Snow White after all. The evil fingers of envy gripped her heart and she knew she would not rest until Snow White was dead.

The queen came up with a horrid idea. She disguised herself as an old pedlar and went to the seven dwarves' house. Knocking on the door she called out,

"Who will buy my beautiful wares? Ribbons and laces in the most gorgeous colours."

Snow White looked out of the window. "I can let an honest old woman in," she thought and unbolted the door. Snow White bought a lace for her bodice from the old woman.

"Oh, my dear," said the pedlar, "you look so pretty. Here, let me lace you in properly."

And before Snow White could answer, the old woman pulled the lace so tightly that Snow White couldn't breathe. She fell to the floor as if dead.

"You used to be the fairest," said the old woman, "but not any more." And with that she left.

As the night fell around the cottage the dwarves returned home. They were shocked to see Snow White lying there on the floor showing no signs of life. Noticing that she could not breathe the dwarves snipped open her bodice lace, and slowly Snow White came round.

When the dwarves found out what had happened they immediately realised who the old woman must

have been. "That was no honest pedlar, but your evil stepmother. Now take care and let no one else in."

At the same time the queen was standing in front of her magic mirror.

"Mirror, mirror, on the wall,

Who is the fairest of them all?"

The mirror replied:

"You are very beautiful my queen, it's true, but Snow White is still a thousand times fairer than you."

When the queen heard that she could barely believe her ears.

"This time," she hissed, "I will make sure that I do the job properly."

Using an evil magic spell the queen made a poisoned comb. Then she disguised herself as another old pedlar woman and sought out the seven dwarves' house. Knocking on the door she cried out:

"Who will buy my beautiful wares?"

"Go away," replied Snow White, "I am not allowed to let anyone in."

"But this comb will be perfect for you," said the old woman, holding it up.

Snow White was so taken with the pretty comb that she forgot the dwarves' warning and unbolted the door to let the old woman in.

"Let me show you how good this comb is," said the old woman. Sitting Snow White down, the woman pulled the comb through her hair. After the first stroke, the poison took effect and Snow White collapsed to the floor.

"Now I shall be the fairest in the land again," cackled the old woman as she left the cottage.

That evening, as the dwarves returned home they were again shocked to find the door open and Snow White slumped on the floor. They immediately suspected that the stepmother had tricked Snow White and searched their friend for clues. They found the comb and once they removed it from Snow White's hair she started to come round.

Back at the castle the queen was standing in front of her mirror.

"Mirror, mirror, on the wall,

Who is the fairest of them all?"

The mirror replied:

"You are very beautiful my queen, it's true,

But Snow White is still a thousand times fairer than you."

The queen exploded with rage. "Snow White will die if it's the last thing I do!"

She went to her chamber, and made a deadly, poisoned apple. From the outside it looked like the most shiny, luscious and tasty apple imaginable, but the smallest bite would kill you. The queen disguised herself again as a pedlar woman and set off through the forest to the dwarves' house.

When the old woman knocked on the door, Snow White stuck her head out of the window and said, "Sorry, I'm not allowed to open the door to anyone."

"Oh, don't worry," said the woman, "I'll get rid of these apples somewhere else. But here, have one anyway."

"Thank you," said Snow White, "But I can't take it."

"What's wrong?" asked the woman. "Afraid it's poisoned? Here, I'll cut it in half. I'll have one half and you can have the other."

Now the apple had been cleverly made, and only the red half was poisoned. The green half was safe. The old woman sliced the apple in two and started to eat the green half. Snow White, seeing the old woman eating the lovely apple gladly took the other half. She had barely bitten into it when she fell to the ground dead.

The old woman looked at her body and laughed. "Even the dwarves can't help you now."

Back home in the castle she went straight to the mirror.

"Mirror, mirror, on the wall,
Who is the fairest of them all?"
The mirror replied:
"You, my queen, are fairest of all."

The dark cloud of envy and hatred retreated and the queen was happy again.

When the dwarves arrived home that night they again found Snow White slumped on the floor. But this time, no matter what they tried to do, they could not bring her round. Snow White was dead.

The dwarves wept for three days. As she looked as beautiful in death as she had in life, the dwarves decided not to bury her, but made a glass coffin so all could see her. They wrote her name on the side in golden letters and put the coffin on the side of the mountain. The dwarves took turns to stay with her and the animals of the forest would also come and watch over the coffin.

The days turned into weeks, the weeks into months and the months into years. But even though the seasons changed, Snow White did not, and she looked as beautiful as the day she died.

It came about that a prince entered the woods looking for shelter and found the dwarves' cottage. He had seen the coffin and was looking for the people who tended it.

"Let me have the coffin and you shall have whatever you desire," he said.

The dwarves refused, saying that the coffin was worth more to them than any gold.

But the prince would not give up. "Then give her to me, for I cannot live without seeing Snow White and will celebrate her beauty for ever."

The dwarves, realising that he was a good man, gave him the coffin. As the prince's servants picked it up they stumbled and the sudden movement dislodged the piece of poisoned apple from Snow White's throat.

Immediately she woke up.

"Where am I?" she asked.

The prince was overjoyed – his cherished love had come to life. "You are with me," he replied. "Come with me to my father's castle and be my wife." Snow White had fallen straight in love with the handsome prince and immediately agreed.

The wedding was planned with great ceremony. Everyone from near and far was invited, even the wicked stepmother.

The evil queen, unaware of who the prince's bride was, dressed in her finest clothes and stepping in front of her mirror, asked:

"Mirror, mirror, on the wall,

Who is the fairest of them all?"

The mirror replied:

"You, my queen, are fair it's true.

But the young queen is a thousand times fairer than you."

The stepmother was enraged. She dashed to the wedding to see exactly who this new queen could be. When she saw it was Snow White she was struck dumb with fear. Turning on her heels she ran and ran, until her very shoes steamed with the heat of it all. And still she ran; and she hasn't been seen since.

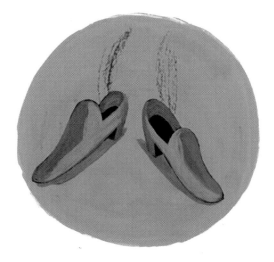

CINDERELLA
OR
THE LITTLE GLASS SLIPPER

There was once a widower, whose wife had borne him a daughter before she had died. This girl had the sweetest of natures, which she had inherited from her mother. Now the man married again, but this time the woman he took as his wife was cold as a winter's day. She had two daughters already and they were as mean-spirited as their mother.

As soon as the wedding was over the second wife showed what she was really like. She had no time for her stepdaughter, as she could see that her goodness and prettiness made her own daughters look even more horrible and ugly in comparison. So the stepmother made the daughter do all of the dirty jobs around the house – washing dishes, scrubbing floors and clearing up after the stepmother and her daughters. The good daughter was forced to sleep on a straw bed in a tiny room in the attic, while the stepmother's daughters had fine rooms and clothes and full-length mirrors to admire themselves in.

The poor girl went about her work patiently, but
with a heavy heart. She couldn't tell her father about
it because he believed everything his new wife told
him. So when the daughter finished her chores, she
just sat amongst the ashes next to the fire in order to
keep warm. Her stepsisters teased her about this and
called her Cinderella. But even though the poor girl
was covered in dirt, she was still more beautiful than
the two ugly sisters in their fine clothes.

Now it happened that the King's son decided to hold a grand ball that would take place over two nights. Every gentleman and lady in the land was invited. The two ugly sisters received their invitations. They spent all day talking about which dress they would wear and what hairstyle to have. Of course while they talked, Cinderella was expected to iron all of their dresses for them to choose which one to wear.

They sent for the best hat-maker in town to design and make them two splendid head-dresses. And Cinderella was consulted in all these matters because she had very good taste, and as she was so sweet-natured she willingly helped her spoilt stepsisters.

As Cinderella was doing the sisters' hair they asked:

"Cinderella, wouldn't you like to go to the ball?"

"No," she replied, "because people would only laugh at me in my tattered clothes."

"Yes, they would, wouldn't they," laughed the sisters. "Imagine a scruff like you at a ball!"

Anyone but Cinderella would have made a bad job of the sisters' hair for being so spiteful, but Cinderella still did her best. Afterwards she could only sit by and watch as the sisters chattered on and on about the ball and tried to make themselves look beautiful. No matter what they wore or how much make-up they put on, they still looked awful. But in their own minds they were beautiful, and went off to the ball sure that they would catch the eye of the young prince.

Cinderella watched her stepsisters leave and then burst out crying. Her godmother saw her crying and asked what was wrong.

"I wish … I wish I could…" but Cinderella was too upset to finish her sentence.

Now this godmother of hers was a fairy, so she knew exactly what was wrong.

"You want to go to the ball, don't you?" she said.

"Yes," sighed Cinderella.

"Well, you deserve to go," said the godmother.

"Now go and fetch me a pumpkin from the garden."

Cinderella went into the garden to find the biggest one she could. The godmother scooped out the entire inside of the pumpkin and then tapped the outside with her wand. Instantly the pumpkin was turned into a beautiful, golden coach.

The godmother then found six mice. She tapped each one with her wand and they were transformed into six fine dappled-grey horses. All that was needed now was a coachman to drive the carriage.

"Would a rat do?" asked Cinderella.

"A rat would be perfect,"
replied her godmother.

Cinderella fetched three rats
and the godmother selected the choicest
and tapped it with her wand. The rat was now
a jolly coachman with a fine moustache.

"Would you go into the garden
again my dear?" the godmother
asked Cinderella. "You'll find six
lizards behind the watering can.
Could you fetch them please?"

No sooner had she brought them than they were
turned into six footmen all dressed in gold and silver.
They lined up behind the coach waiting for the off.

"Now my dear, it's your turn," said the godmother. Cinderella's rags were turned into a fabulous ballgown covered in sparkling jewels. Finally the godmother conjured up a pair of glass slippers, which must have been the prettiest shoes in the land.

Now everything was ready. Cinderella climbed into the carriage but, before she left, her godmother warned her not to stay after midnight, for after that time the coach would become a pumpkin again, the horses mice, the coachman a rat, her footmen lizards and her fine clothes would again be rags.

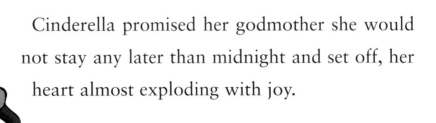

Cinderella promised her godmother she would not stay any later than midnight and set off, her heart almost exploding with joy.

When the king's son saw her arrive he imagined she must be a grand princess. He rushed out to meet Cinderella, helped her out of her carriage and led her to the ball. When they entered the ballroom everyone fell silent, so struck were they with the beauty of the mysterious woman with the prince. Even the king remarked to his wife on Cinderella's beauty, and all the ladies there noted the cut of her dress so they might copy it later.

The prince led Cinderella to her seat, but then spent most of the evening dancing with her. Cinderella was so elegant on the dance floor that the other guests

could not help but admire her all the more. When the banquet was served the prince didn't eat a mouthful as he spent all his time gazing at the beautiful stranger.

Cinderella spotted her two stepsisters and went across to talk to them. Of course the sisters, like everyone else, failed to recognize Cinderella, but this is not really surprising as they were so caught up in their own lives they never really knew what Cinderella looked like. This amused Cinderella a great deal, but as she was talking she heard the clock strike a quarter to twelve. She politely excused herself and quickly left the ball.

When she got home, Cinderella dashed straight to her godmother and thanked her. As she was telling her godmother all about the ball, she heard the front door open and her two stepsisters come in.

"Oh you've been out a long time," said Cinderella rubbing her eyes pretending she had been asleep.

"If you'd been at the ball you wouldn't have slept," replied the sisters. "There was a beautiful princess there, nearly as pretty as us. She was very nice, too and talked to us for ages."

"And what was her name?" asked Cinderella.

"No one knows, and the prince would give the world to find out."

At this Cinderella smiled. "Oh I'd love to see her for myself. May I borrow some of your clothes so I could go tonight?"

"Lend you some clothes?" cried one sister.

"To a scruff bag like you?" cried the other.

"Don't be so silly!" they chorused.

Cinderella knew this would be their answer and smiled quietly to herself.

The next evening the stepsisters went off to the ball again; and so did Cinderella. This time she looked even more magnificent than the previous night. The prince never left her side and they danced and talked and danced some more.

Cinderella was having the time of her life and quite forgot her godmother's warning. In fact she had so lost track of the time that when the clock struck twelve it caught her completely by surprise. Without as much as a goodbye she jumped up and ran off out of the ballroom. The prince got up to follow but Cinderella had been as nimble as a deer and there was no sign of her anywhere. All that was left was one of her glass slippers which she had dropped in her hurry.

When Cinderella got home she was already in her usual rags with no trace of her finery left, apart from one glass slipper that did not change back because it had been separated from the other shoe.

Meanwhile the prince was quizzing his guards about the missing princess. The only woman the guards had seen was a young peasant girl dressed in filthy rags.

When the two sisters returned from the ball Cinderella asked them if they had enjoyed themselves and whether the mysterious princess was there.

"Yes, she was," they replied. "But she hurried away at midnight and dropped one of her pretty glass slippers. The prince picked it up, and you could tell by the way he was moping about he was in love with the shoe's owner."

And what they said was true, for three days later there was a royal proclamation that the prince would marry whoever fitted inside the glass slipper he had in his possession. A gentleman was sent from court with the slipper to find the woman whose foot would fit the shoe.

He started with all of the princesses, then the duchesses, and all the ladies, but nobody's foot would fit the slipper. Eventually the slipper was brought to the two ugly sisters. They squeezed their feet into the slipper, but of course it didn't fit.

Cinderella watched all this from the corner, knowing it was her shoe.

"Let me try, please," she said.

At this the two stepsisters fell about laughing.

"Don't listen to the stupid girl," they told the gentleman, "it can't possibly fit her."

But the gentleman had a wise head on his shoulders and noticed that, beneath all the dirt, Cinderella was a beautiful lady. He asked her to sit down and slid the slipper onto her foot. Of course it was a perfect fit.

Cinderella then pulled the other slipper from her pocket and put it on her other foot.

Cinderella's godmother appeared and touched her with the wand and Cinderella's rags were transformed into clothes more beautiful than anything she had worn before.

Seeing that Cinderella was indeed the mysterious princess, her stepsisters fell to their knees begging for forgiveness for all the terrible things they had done to her. Cinderella, being the sweet-natured girl she was, gathered the sisters to her and forgave them and asked that they should love her always.

Cinderella was taken to the young prince, who was overjoyed to see her again. They were married a few days later and Cinderella, proving that she had no malice in her heart, found two fine gentlemen for her stepsisters to marry, too.

SLEEPING BEAUTY

There was once a king and queen who had no children. This made them very sad. For years they tried every potion and cure possible in order to help, but to no avail. So you can imagine their joy when the queen unexpectedly gave birth to a baby girl.

To celebrate they organised the finest christening there had ever been. The king and queen invited every fairy in the land to be godmothers and, as was the custom at the time, each of them was to give the child a magical gift.

After the ceremony everyone returned to the King's palace where a great feast had been prepared for the fairies. In front of every fairy was placed a plate with magnificent gold cover over it. The knife, fork and spoon were also made of gold and inlaid with rubies. But just as they were about to start eating, an old fairy entered the room. She had not been invited because no one had seen her for over fifty years and she was presumed dead or gone to a different land.

The king immediately ordered a place to be set for her. However she could not be given a plate with a golden case or any jewel-encrusted cutlery as they had been made specially for the godmothers. The old fairy was put out by this and muttered under her breath. One of the godmothers heard the old fairy mumbling and guessed she meant to give the baby an unlucky gift. So the godmother left the table and hid herself away in order that she would be the last one to give the baby her gift and so undo whatever mischief the old fairy might cause.

In the meantime the other fairy godmothers had begun to give their gifts to the baby princess. One gave her the gift of beauty, another gave her wit, another gave her grace, the fourth gave her the ability to dance beautifully, the fifth the singing voice of an angel, and the sixth that she should be musically talented and be able to play any instrument.

Then the old fairy came to the crib, still seething with rage and spite. Glaring at the poor child, she said that the princess would prick her finger on a spindle and die from the wound. When the assembled guests heard this horrid gift they wept as if the baby had died there and then.

At this moment the last godmother appeared from her hiding place. She was not powerful enough to undo the old fairy's evil magic completely, but she could alter it.

"The princess will prick her hand, it's true," she said, "but she will not die. Instead she shall sleep for a hundred years and be awoken by the kiss of a prince."

The king also tried to prevent the old fairy's spell from happening by immediately forbidding anyone in the kingdom to own a spindle.

All was well for the next sixteen years. Then one day, when the king and queen were away from the palace, the young princess amused herself by exploring some of the rooms she had not yet visited. At the very top of a tower she came upon a small room in which an old woman worked at her spindle. This good woman had never heard the king's proclamation banning spindles.

"What are you doing?" asked the princess.

"I'm spinning, my pretty child," said the old woman, who did not know who the princess was.

"That looks like fun," said the princess. "May I have a go?"

She was in such a hurry to try her hand at spinning that she pricked her finger on the spindle. Immediately the princess fell to the floor in a deep faint. The old woman cried for help and soon the room was filled with people trying to revive the princess. They threw cold water on her, slapped her hands and rubbed her temples, but nothing could wake the princess.

Meanwhile the king had returned. Seeing what had come to pass and realising the fairy's predictions had come true he arranged for the princess to be taken to her chambers and laid upon her bed. She looked as if she might wake at any moment so alive did she look, but her breathing was very soft and the poor king knew she would be like this for one hundred years.

Now the good fairy that had saved her life by changing the old fairy's spell was in a different kingdom, but she heard of the accident almost immediately. A dwarf who had a pair of boots that allowed him to travel seven leagues with every step had dashed to tell the fairy as soon as the terrible events had unfolded. The fairy returned with him to the palace straight away.

The fairy already knew what she had to do. The princess would be at a loss when she awoke, for all the people she remembered from before her sleep would be dead. So the fairy touched every living thing in the palace with her wand, except the king and queen. Everyone that the fairy touched fell

into a deep, deep sleep.
They too would sleep for a
hundred years and would wake when the
princess did, ready to serve her. The king and
queen preferred to stay awake so that they
could watch over their child for as long as
they might live.

The king and queen kissed their child then ordered that nobody should come near the palace. The fairy then cast a spell that made thick brambles, trees and plants grow around the palace, until the building was almost completely hidden from view.

A hundred winters came and went and no-one went near the palace. Then one day a young prince went hunting near the overgrown palace.

Noticing the towers poking through the vegetation the prince asked some passing peasants:

"What building is that in the middle of the wood?"
"It's an old castle haunted by ghosts," said one.
"A meeting place for witches," said another.
"An ogre who eats children lives there," said yet another.

The prince didn't know who to believe. Then the last member of the group spoke to him.

"If it pleases your highness," said the good man, "I heard from my father, who heard from his father, that a princess has slept there for a hundred years waiting for the kiss of a prince to wake her."

The prince was seized by a sudden passion. If it was a prince that was needed then he would answer the call, and off he raced towards the overgrown palace!

He found that he could slice his way through the thick plants with ease, almost as if they were moving apart for him. When he looked back he saw that no one could follow him – the plants closed up again after he had passed. Although this surprised him, he continued on his way.

Eventually he reached the palace and was amazed by what he saw. All around were the stretched out bodies of people and animals as if they were dead. But he could see by the people's healthy complexions that they were not dead but sleeping. Everything was just

as it was when they had fallen asleep. Their food was still preserved on their plates and there was still drink in their cups.

He went through many rooms including a guards' room with a line of soldiers asleep with their muskets, and various chambers filled with both gentlemen and ladies. Some were standing, some were sitting, but all were asleep. Finally he came upon a room with a bed in the middle of it. And on the bed was the finest young woman he had ever seen, a beautiful princess who radiated goodness and generosity.

He approached the bed and fell to his knees at its side. The prince lent over and gently kissed the princess on the lips. The evil spell was broken and the princess opened her eyes.

"Is it you, my Prince?" she said to him.

The Prince's heart overflowed with joy when he heard the princess speak. He assured her that all was well and admitted that he had already fallen hopelessly in love with her. They talked and wept as they got to know each other. And though history does not record what they said, perhaps the princess told him of the wonderful dreams the good fairy had given her during her sleep. For in those dreams she had seen this very prince.

In the meantime, the rest of the palace began to come to life. Naturally, after so long asleep, everyone was very hungry. The lady in waiting, being more impatient than most, told the prince that supper was served. The prince helped the princess to dress and had the good manners not to point out that her clothes were no longer fashionable.

They went into the great hall where they ate and were entertained by musicians playing tunes that had not been heard for the last hundred years. Straight after supper, the prince and princess married in the palace chapel.

The next morning the prince left for the city, where his father was waiting for him, wondering why he had not returned that night. The prince told him that he had lost his way while hunting and had spent the night at a peasant's house where he had been fed bread and cheese.

The king was a trusting man, so believed his son's story; but his wife would not be convinced it was true. And she grew more suspicious when the prince went hunting at every opportunity and was away for three or four days at a time. She began to suspect that he had secretly got married.

The prince continued to live like this for two years. In that time the princess gave birth to two children. The oldest, a girl, they named Aurore, which means dawn, for she was as beautiful as the early morning. The second, a boy, they named Day, for he was even more handsome than his sister.

The prince's mother often asked her son what he was up to while he was away. The prince was scared to tell her though. His mother

was an ogress, being from the land of the ogres. His father would never have married her had she not been extremely wealthy. It was even whispered around court that the queen still had ogreish tendencies, and had to struggle not eat little children on sight. So the prince breathed not one word about his wife and children.

Two years later, the king died and the prince became king in his place. This also meant his wife was now queen. The new king told everyone about his secret marriage and brought his queen back to his palace in great ceremony. They made a magnificent entry into the city with the queen riding between her two children.

It came to pass that the king was forced to go to war with the Emperor Contalabutte, ruler of the neighbouring land. The king left the running of the country to his mother and instructed her to take care of his wife and children. No sooner had the king left than his mother sent them to live in a house amongst the woods; for the mother had evil plans afoot. She was, after all, from the land of the ogres. A few days later the mother arrived at the country house herself and said to the head butler:

"I have a mind to eat little Aurore, today."

"No, madam!" cried the butler.

"I will have it so! And I shall have her with a cheese sauce," replied the fearsome ogress.

The poor butler knew not to cross an ogress. He picked up a knife and went to Aurore's chamber. The little girl was four years old and as beautiful as the day she was born. She jumped for joy when she saw the butler, hugged him and asked if he had any sweets.

At this the butler burst into tears and fled the room. He went out into the fields and killed a lamb instead, had it cooked and covered with the most delicious

cheese sauce and served to the ogress. She devoured it all, telling him she had tasted nothing finer all her life. While she was eating, the butler smuggled away Aurore and hid her in

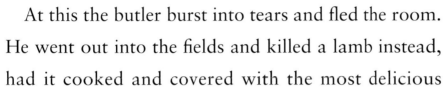

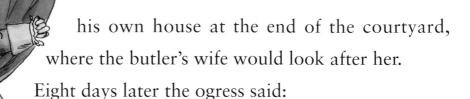

his own house at the end of the courtyard, where the butler's wife would look after her.

Eight days later the ogress said:

"I have a mind to eat little Day for dinner."

This time the butler knew what to do. He went to Day's room where the boy was enjoying a great battle with a toy monkey. The butler took the boy in his arms and carried him to his house at the end of the courtyard where Day joined his sister. Then the butler killed a young goat, had it cooked and presented it to the ogress who enjoyed it immensely.

Everything seemed to be going well, until the ogress came to the head butler one evening.

"I have a mind to eat the new queen with the same

delicious sauce as I had over her children."

The butler despaired. The queen was over twenty years old, not including the hundred years she had been asleep; where would he find an animal with meat that firm? He resolved that the only way to save his own life was to carry out the ogress' orders. He marched up to the queen's chambers. He was not going to surprise her, but respectfully told the queen why he had come and that he was following the orders given to him by the queen's mother-in-law.

"Then do it," said the queen, stretching out her neck to receive the knife. "Follow your orders and then I shall be able to see my poor children whom I loved so dearly." The queen had also thought that her children were dead, as they had been taken without her knowledge.

"No, no madam," cried the butler in tears. "I shall not do it. Come with me to my lodgings, for I have hidden your children there. I shall try to deceive the ogress once more by giving her a deer instead."

They did just that, and the ogress ate the deer believing it to be the young queen. She found it as delicious as the other two meals. Being a devious sort, she had already thought of how she would explain the disappearance of the queen and her children to her son, the king. She would say whilst dabbing her tearful eyes that they had all been eaten by wolves that were common in those parts.

The next evening the ogress was taking a walk around the grounds when she heard a noise. She could have sworn it was the voice of the young queen telling off Day and Aurore, who were crying noisily. The queen and her children were still alive! The ogress was furious at being deceived.

At dawn the next day she ordered that a huge cauldron be brought into the middle of the courtyard. This she had filled with toads, poisonous snakes, and all sorts of foul creatures. The ogress then ordered that the queen, her children, the head butler and his wife be brought to her with their hands tied behind them.

All of those people were rounded up and brought before the ogress. They were about to be thrown into the cauldron when the king arrived. He was horrified by what he saw

and demanded to know what was going on. The ogress was horrified to have been caught out like this. Knowing there was no way of getting away with what she was doing she flung herself head first into the cauldron. She was immediately devoured by all the vile creatures which she had put in there. The king could not help but be upset by this, for the ogress was his mother after all. But knowing that he had saved his beloved wife and children was a bigger comfort to him, and from that day on he promised never to leave their side again.

There once was a poor miller who had three sons. When the miller died all he left to his sons was a mill, a donkey, and a cat. The eldest son had the mill, the second took the donkey and the third had the cat.

The youngest son was very sad.

"My brothers can make a living by using the mill and the donkey. But for me, all I have is this cat and what use is that?"

"Do not worry master," said the cat. "All you have to do is get me a bag and have me a pair boots made so I can scramble through the dirt and brambles. Then you'll see that your inheritance will serve you well."

Now the son knew the cat was very cunning, for he had seen him use the cleverest of tricks to catch rats. So the son felt slightly cheered by the cat's speech and wondered what the cat had in mind.

When the cat got what he had asked for he pulled on his boots and slung the bag around his neck. He went out into the fields and filled the bag with the tastiest of plants, then, stretching out on the ground as if he were dead, held the bag in his paw.

Just as the cat had planned, a young rabbit was soon sniffing around the bag, for rabbits like nothing better than tasty plants. The rabbit jumped into the bag and, quick as a flash, the cat tied the bag shut. Now if you expected the cat to take the bag to the son then you are wrong. Instead the cat took the bag to the king.

Marching into the king's apartments, the cat made a low bow and said to him.

"Your majesty, I have brought you a rabbit which my master, the Marquis of Carabas (which is the name the cat had given to the son) has commanded me to present to you."

"Tell your master," said the king, "that I thank him very much, for I am fond of rabbit."

The cat left and hid himself in a corn field. He held the bag wide open and in no time a couple of partridges, which are stupid birds, had run right into the bag. Quick as a flash the cat tied the bag and went to see the king as before. The king was overjoyed with his new gift and gave the cat some money for his troubles.

Now the cat continued to do this for a couple of months and soon he learnt all of the king's habits. Knowing that the king often went for a carriage ride by the river with his beautiful daughter, the cat said to his master:

"If you want to earn your fortune, go and wash yourself in the river where I tell you. Leave the rest to me."

While the son was washing, the king passed by. The cat cried out:

"Help! Help! My lord, the Marquis of Carabas is drowning!"

Hearing the noise the king poked his head through the carriage window. Seeing that it was the cat who was shouting, and believing the miller's son to be a marquis, the king ordered his guards to help the son. As they pulled him out of the river, the cat walked up to the coach.

"Thank you, your majesty," said the cat. "While my master was washing, some thieves stole his clothes and he was in no position to chase after them."

Now the cat had cleverly hidden the miller's son's clothes underneath a rock. Seeing that the son was naked the king ordered his guards to bring him a suit from the palace.

The suit, when it arrived, fitted the son very well. It was a very fine suit and the son, being a good-looking boy beneath all the dirt, looked quite dashing overall.

It was no surprise that the king's daughter fell in love with him there and then.

The king invited the son to join them in his coach. As they rode along, the cat marched a good distance ahead. The cat, spying some peasants mowing a meadow, cried out:

"Good people of the fields, if you do not tell the king these fields belong to the Marquis of Carabas, I shall have you chopped into pieces."

Now the cat knew that the king liked to ask questions of everyone he passed on his rides. And sure enough, when the king passed the peasants he asked them who the field belonged to.

"To my lord, the Marquis of Carabas," they replied, for they believed if a cat was wearing boots it must be quite important and should be listened to.

"Yes your majesty," said the miller's son spotting the cat's plan, "this meadow produces a fine harvest every year."

The cat continued on ahead of the carriage. Seeing some workers harvesting some corn, he cried out:

"Good people of the fields, if you do not tell the king these fields belong to the Marquis of Carabas, I shall have you chopped into pieces."

And when the king passed the workers he asked them who the field belonged to.

"To my lord, the Marquis of Carabas," they replied, for they also believed if a cat was wearing boots it must be quite important and should be listened to.

The king was very impressed by the workers' answer and congratulated the son on owning so much fine land.

Eventually the cat came to a huge and imposing castle. It belonged to a fierce ogre who also owned all the fields which the cat had passed on the way. The cat knew full well who the castle belonged to and asked at the gate if he could pay his respects to the ogre.

The cat was shown in to a large room where the ogre was seated.

"Good day, Sir," said the cat. "I have been told that you have the ability to change yourself into any shape you desire, such as an elephant or a lion for example."

"Yes, it's true," replied the ogre brusquely. "And to prove it I shall now become a lion."

And in a flash the ogre had become a fearsome lion. The cat took such a fright at the sight that he hightailed it onto the roof, and

refused to come down until the ogre had changed back into his usual form.

"I have been told," said the cat, "that you can also turn yourself into the smallest of animals such as a rat or a mouse for example. However I think that must be impossible."

"Impossible?" roared the ogre. "Nothing is impossible for me."

And quick as a flash the ogre changed into a mouse; but just as quickly the cat pounced on him and ate him.

Just at that moment, the king's carriage pulled up outside the castle. The king was just about to enquire as to whom such a splendid castle might belong when the cat appeared at the gate.

"Your majesty," said the cat, "welcome to the castle of the Marquis of Carabas."

"My lord Marquis!" cried the king. "What a fine castle, it must be the grandest in the land. May I look around?"

The king, the miller's son and the king's daughter all trooped into the castle. The king was overcome by the fine chambers and was convinced that the Marquis must be the most splendid of gentlemen. So did the king's daughter who, since the carriage ride, was head over heels in love with the miller's son.

Seeing his daughter's obvious love for the boy, the king turned to the miller's son and said,

"My dear Marquis, I insist you become my son-in-law. Will you marry my daughter?"

The miller's son accepted of course, and he and the king's daughter were married that very day.

LITTLE THUMB

Once upon a time there was a man and a wife with seven children, all boys. The oldest was ten years-old and the youngest seven. The family was very poor and the children were too young to work, so when the seventh child had been born it was a great worry for the parents. What concerned the parents more was that this youngest child hardly uttered a word and, worse still, he was tiny. When he was born he was no bigger than a thumb and this was why they called him Little Thumb.

This poor child always got the blame when something went wrong in the house, whether it was his fault or not. However the little lad was more cunning than all his brothers put together, and though he didn't speak much he was very good at listening and learning from those around him.

Now one year there was a very bad harvest and the people went hungry. There was no option for the poor but to get rid of their children or they would all starve to death.

One evening, when all their children were in bed, the man said to his wife:

"We have so little food that we can no longer keep our children. I cannot watch them starve, so I shall lose them in the woods tomorrow."

The mother would not agree to her husband's idea. However when she thought of how terrible it would be to watch them starve in front of her, she reluctantly agreed to her husband's plan. She then went to bed in tears. Little did they know that someone had overheard them talking. Little Thumb had been awake and had crept under his father's stool to hear what they were saying. He then went back to bed and lay awake working out what to do.

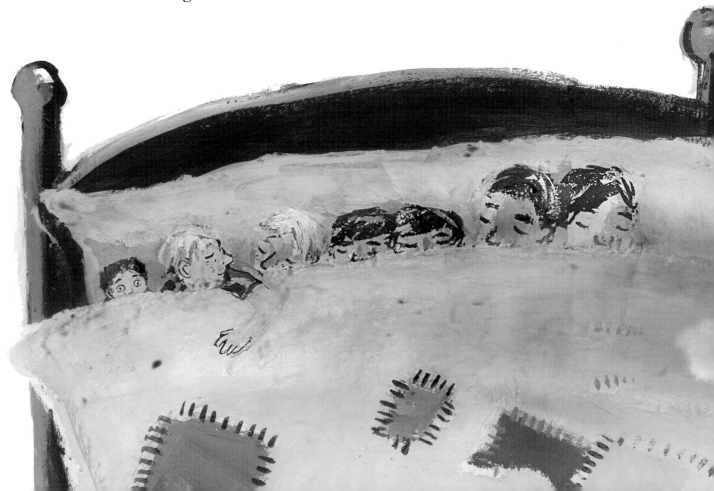

Early the next morning Little Thumb got up before anyone else, went out to the river, and filled his pockets with little white stones and then came back home. Later the whole family went deep into the forest to collect firewood. The father and mother waited until the children were busy picking up sticks, then ran away back through the forest.

When the children saw they were all alone they began to cry, except for Little Thumb. On his way into the forest he had dropped those little white stones to leave a trail, so he knew he could get the children back

home. He beckoned for his siblings to follow and took them all home. They did not go indoors though, but instead listened at the door to what their parents were saying.

Now as it happened, when their parents had got home the local landowner had sent them ten gold coins which he had owed them for some time. This was a most welcome surprise and the couple immediately went to the butchers and bought a great deal of food. The meal was all the tastier for them being so hungry before it.

When they had finished the woman said:

"Oh, but our poor children, what has become of them? They would have made a feast of what we have left here. I told you that no good would come of this. They've probably been eaten by wolves. You are inhuman for abandoning your children."

The husband started to get angry as his wife repeated her lament about twenty times. He was proud of the fact that his wife could speak so

eloquently, but preferred it when she did not direct her tongue at him. By now she was half-drowned in tears crying out:

"Oh where are my children, my poor children?"

Of course the children were outside the door and could hear every word. They cried out together:

"Here we are, here we are!"

The wife ran to the door and opened it. Hugging her children she said:

"Oh I'm so glad to see you. You look so hungry, and Peter you look so dirty. Come in here and let me clean you up."

Now Peter was the eldest son and was his mother's favourite because he had ginger hair just as she did. She ushered them all to the table and the children ate their fill. The parents were happy to have the children home, and this joy continued until the ten gold coins were all spent. Then times became hard again and the parents decided they would have to lose the children again. This time they resolved to take the children much further away than before.

Fortunately for the boys, Little Thumb had overheard his parents' plans again. But this time when Little Thumb tried to leave the house in the early morning he found the door locked and double-bolted. He was at a loss about what to do until breakfast time. All the children were given a small loaf of bread, so Little Thumb kept his loaf, planning to use it to leave a trail of bread.

The father and mother led their children into the thickest part of the forest and again left them there to fend for themselves. Little Thumb was not too worried for he had left a trail of crumbs; so you can imagine his surprise when he discovered that the birds had eaten every

single crumb. The children were now all alone with little hope of finding their way back to their house.

Night fell and a strong wind blew through the trees. The children imagined they heard the howling of wolves all around them and were very afraid. To make matters worse it started to rain and soon they were all soaked to the skin. The children were cold, wet, afraid and all alone in the dark forest.

Little Thumb climbed to the top of a tall tree to see if he could see anything. In the distance he could make

out a light flickering, but it seemed to come from beyond the forest. Of course when he climbed down the tree he could no longer see it, but luck was with them and eventually they came to the house that had been the source of the light. They knocked at the door which was opened by a friendly woman.

Little Thumb explained that they were poor children who had been left in the forest and were looking for somewhere to shelter for the night.

At this news the woman began to weep.

"Oh my poor children," she said, "why did you come here? This house is owned by an ogre who eats little children."

"What shall we do?" asked Little Thumb. "If we go back to the forest the wolves will surely eat us. I think I would rather try our luck with the ogre; he may take pity on us, especially if you beg him too."

The ogre's wife believed she might be able to hide the children until morning and let them in. They warmed themselves by the fire over which a sheep was roasting for the ogre's supper.

They had just begun to
get warmed through when they heard
three or four great raps upon the door. It was
the ogre returning for his supper. The wife hid the
children under the bed and went to open the door.
The ogre sat at the table and demanded his supper.
The sheep had been roasting for the smallest amount
of time and was still raw and bloody; but the ogre
preferred it this way.

"I smell fresh meat," he growled.

"I killed a calf earlier, it must be that," replied his wife.

"Fresh meat I tell you, still alive!"

With that the ogre got up and went over to the bed.

"Ah I see!" said the ogre. "Trying to cheat me were you? I should eat you up too, but you'd probably make a tough old joint of meat. I've got three ogres of my acquaintance coming to see me in a day or two, and these here will make a fine meal."

With that he dragged the children out one by one from under the bed. They begged for mercy, but their pleas fell on deaf ears. Instead the ogre decided to eat one of the children there and then. He told his wife to prepare a savoury sauce while he sharpened a knife.

He picked up one of the children ready to kill him when the wife said:

"Why do that now? There's plenty of time tomorrow."

"Hush woman!" he replied. "They're nice and tender at the moment."

"But why do you need more meat?" asked his wife. "There's plenty here already."

"That's true," said the ogre. "We'll fatten the children up and put them to bed."

The woman was overjoyed to hear this. She made the children supper, but the boys were too frightened to eat any of it. As for the ogre, he was so happy at finding this unexpected feast he drank too much wine and had to go to bed.

Now the ogre had seven young daughters. They all liked fresh meat like their father, but had little grey eyes, hooked noses, and long sharp teeth. They were quite mischievous and had already started to bite children to suck their

blood. Little Thumb and his brothers slept in a big bed in the same room as the ogresses.

Little Thumb was worried that the ogre might change his mind and try to eat the children during the night. Noticing that the ogresses had little gold crowns upon their heads, Little Thumb had an idea. He gently removed each crown and put them on his own head and his brothers'. Then he settled back into bed and waited.

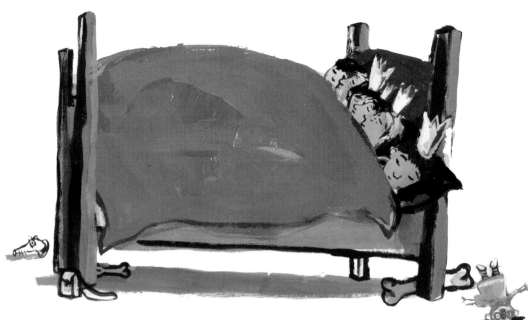

Later that night the ogre woke up feeling a bit peckish. Remembering that there were seven little children in the house he fetched his knife to get himself a midnight snack.

The ogre stumbled into his daughters' room, and felt around for the boys. The first thing he felt was seven little crowns.

"Ah, not this bed," mumbled the ogre to himself, his head still thick with wine.

Then he went to the bed where his daughters lay.

"Ah, here we are," he said. "Well let us get to work."

And the ogre cut the throats of all seven of his daughters. However he did not have time to eat any of them as all the wine he had drunk was beginning to make him feel sick. Instead he went back to bed happy in the knowledge that a fine breakfast awaited him.

As soon as Little Thumb heard the ogre snoring

again he woke his brothers and got them to follow him out of the house and over the garden wall. They kept running all night, not knowing where they were going.

When the ogre woke the next morning he asked his wife to fetch the small children. Of course the wife had no idea what had happened that night and was expecting to go upstairs to bring down the small boys. Imagine how she felt when instead she saw her seven daughters dead in their bed. The shock was too much for the woman and she fainted.

The ogre wondered what was keeping his wife so went to the room himself to find out what was going on. He was horrified by what he saw.

"What have I done?" he cried. "Those wretches will pay for this!"

He woke his wife and said:

"Bring me my seven league boots and I'll catch them in no time."

The ogre covered a great deal of ground searching this way and that and eventually came to the very road which the children were on, not a hundred paces from their father's house. The children had seen the ogre approach, stepping from

mountain to mountain and over great rivers as if they were trickles. Little Thumb spotted a hollow rock to the side of the road and ushered his brothers inside it.

By this point the ogre was very tired, for seven league boots exhaust their wearer. He decided to take a rest and sat himself down on a rock – the very rock the children had hidden in. He soon fell asleep and began to snore. The noise was so bad that it frightened the children as much as anything else on their adventure. Little Thumb however was not nearly as frightened as his brothers and told them that they

should run home while the ogre was asleep. The brothers did not need telling twice and dashed home.

Little Thumb went up to the ogre and gently pulled off his boots. Now seven league boots are doubly magical for they will fit any wearer, so Little Thumb had no difficulty in wearing the boots, too. He went immediately to the ogre's house, where the wife was weeping for her dead daughters.

"Your husband has been captured by a gang of thieves and is in great danger," said Little Thumb. "They have sworn to kill him if he does not give them all his gold and silver. He spotted me and asked me to come and tell you about his predicament and that you should give me everything he has of value. As this news is urgent he gave me his seven league boots to speed me on my journey."

The good woman gave him everything they had, which was a great deal as they were very wealthy. Then Little Thumb took everything back to his father's house and was received like a returning hero.

Now there are some people who disagree with my telling of the story. They claim that Little Thumb never robbed the ogre and say that he merely kept the seven league boots to stop the ogre chasing children. They say that Little Thumb had gone to the palace instead and saw the king. There he was informed that the country was at war and no one knew what had happened to a certain army which was two hundred leagues away. Little Thumb was said to have told the king that if it was desired he would go and bring him back news of his army.

Little Thumb

The king offered Little Thumb a handsome reward and Little Thumb was as good as his word. As he wore the magical boots he returned that very night and was well paid for carrying the news. They also claim Little Thumb acted as a messenger for the king for a while longer and became very wealthy as a result before returning to his father. His wealth made life very easy for the family and he bought houses for his parents and all his brothers. And the family then lived very comfortably till the end of their days.

LITTLE RED RIDING HOOD

Once upon a time there lived a little girl whose grandmother had made her a bright red riding cape with a hood to protect the girl's head from the wind and rain. The girl wore her cape every day, so people started calling her Little Red Riding Hood.

One day her mother said:

"Your grandmother is feeling a bit under the weather. Take her these cakes to cheer her up."

So Little Red Riding Hood set off to visit her grandmother, who lived in the middle of the forest.

As she skipped down the path she was spotted by a big, bad wolf. Now the wolf liked eating children more than anything else on earth and thought Little Red Riding Hood would make an especially tasty meal. He couldn't eat her now because she was too close to the village, so he sidled up to her instead and asked where she was going.

Now Little Red Riding Hood didn't know it was dangerous to speak to wolves, so she replied:

"I'm off to see my grandmother. She isn't very well."

"And where does your grandmother live?" asked the wolf.

"She lives in the house in the middle of the forest," replied Little Red Riding Hood.

"Really?" said the wolf. "Well do give her my love." And off he scampered into the forest.

Now wolves can run much faster than girls can skip, so the wolf arrived at grandmother's house long before Little Red Riding Hood. The wolf knocked at the door.

"Who's there?" asked the old woman.

"It's Little Red Riding Hood," replied the wolf in a high voice. "I've brought you some cakes."

"That's nice dear," said the old woman. "Let yourself in, will you, as I'm still in bed."

The wolf opened the door and seeing that the grandmother was indeed in bed, jumped on her and ate her. Then, pulling on the old woman's nightclothes, lay in her bed and waited for Little Red Riding Hood.

Soon there came a knock at the door.

"Who's there?" asked the wolf in a croaky voice, pretending to be the old woman.

"It's Little Red Riding Hood," replied the girl. "I've brought you some cakes from Mama."

"That's nice dear," said the wolf. "Let yourself in, will you, as I'm still in bed."

As Little Red Riding Hood came in the wolf snuggled right down into the bed so the little girl wouldn't notice who it was.

"Come closer my dear so I can see you," said the wolf.

Little Red Riding Hood took off her cape and sat on the edge of the bed. She was shocked to see the way her grandmother looked, and imagined she must be very ill.

"Grandma, what big ears you have," said Little Red Riding Hood.

"All the better to hear you with, my dear," replied the wolf.

"Grandma, what big eyes you have," said Little Red Riding Hood.

"All the better to see you with, my dear," replied the wolf.

"Grandma, what big teeth you have," said Little Red Riding Hood.

"All the better to eat you with, my dear!" cried the wolf. And with that he lunged at Little Red Riding Hood, meaning to gobble her up.

Little Red Riding Hood let out a piercing shriek and tried to flee. Luckily a passing woodcutter heard her cries and came rushing into the cottage. With one swing of his mighty axe he chopped the wicked wolf in two – and from its belly jumped out Grandma, alive and well.

THE UGLY DUCKLING

It was a gorgeous summer's day in the country and the golden corn and the green oats nodded their heads lazily in the sunshine. The fields and meadows were surrounded by large forests with deep pools, and in the sunniest spot in the forest stood an old farmhouse nestled by the side of a deep, slow river. At the edge of the river grew huge burdock leaves, tall enough for a child to hide in with ease.

In the middle of these leaves was a mother duck. She was on her nest waiting impatiently for her ducklings to hatch. They were taking their time about it and the mother was getting a bit bored. The other ducks were all splashing about on the river and the mother very much wanted to join them.

Eventually one egg cracked, and then another, and another until all but one of the eggs had hatched. The little ducklings stuck their heads out of their shells and said, "Peep, peep."

"No," said their mother,

"quack, quack."

And all of the ducklings said "quack, quack," as best they could. Then they climbed out of their eggs and peeped through the huge burdock leaves.

"How big the world is!" they said, for the garden was much bigger than their eggs.

"Do you think that's all there is to the world?" said their mother. "Beyond the garden are huge fields and meadows, too. Now are you all out? Ah, no, the large egg still hasn't hatched."

And with a sigh, the mother duck settled herself back on her nest and waited for it to hatch.

"Still on the nest?" cried an old duck as he walked past later.

"Waiting for the last one to hatch," replied the mother. "But look at my other ducklings, aren't they the finest you've ever seen?"

"Let me see the egg," said the old duck. "It's probably a turkey's egg. I was asked to hatch some once, but no matter what I did, I couldn't encourage those chicks to go anywhere near the water. They couldn't even quack. Yes, that's a turkey egg. Take my advice, just leave it where it is and go and teach those ducklings of yours to swim."

"I'll sit on it for a little while longer," replied the mother. "I've waited this long that a couple more days won't make the slightest difference."

"Well, suit yourself," answered the old duck and he waddled off.

Eventually, the large egg broke open and a little head popped out shouting "Peep, peep." Sadly, it was a very large and very ugly-looking duckling.

"Oh my," thought the mother, "it doesn't look much like the others. I do hope it's not a turkey after all. I know, tomorrow I'll see if it can swim."

The next day the weather was beautiful again and the sun warmed the burdock leaves that were home to the ducks. The mother took her ducklings down to the river and jumped in with a splash. "Quack, quack," she cried and each of her ducklings popped into the river in turn. After a brief bit of splashing they were paddling around the water as if they had been doing it for years. And the big, ugly duckling was right there with them.

"Oh, so he's not a turkey, after all," thought his mother. And because mothers think their babies are beautiful she quite forgot how ugly a duckling he really was.

"Quack, quack. Follow me my babies and I'll introduce you to the animals of the farmyard, though do watch out for the cat."

As they entered the farmyard, two families were fighting there over an eel's head. As they argued the cat slunk by and made off with the head.

"See, that is the way of the world," said the mother, who would have quite liked the eel's head herself. "Now, stand up straight and don't turn your toes in – well-bred ducks walk with the feet spread wide. And make sure you bow your heads to the old duck in the corner and say 'quack', for he is the most regal duck in the whole farmyard. He has Spanish blood you know."

As the ducklings walked through the farmyard, the other ducks stopped fighting and looked at them.

"Not more ducklings!" one of them exclaimed. "As if there weren't enough of us already. And look at that big one. Now that's an ugly duckling. We don't want the likes of him here."

And with that he bit the ugly duckling on the neck.

"Stop that," said the duckling's mother. "What's he done to you?"

"But he's so ugly. He's simply got to go."

"What a shame," said the old duck, "the others are such pretty ducklings. Can't you do anything with him?"

"I'm afraid not, sir," replied the mother. "He may not be the prettiest, but he's a fine swimmer. And it's not really his fault; he was just in the egg too long. I'm sure he'll get prettier as he gets older." She stroked the duckling's neck where it had been nipped. "Besides he's a drake, so as long as he grows up strong his looks are neither here nor there."

"Well, the other ducklings are fine enough," said the old duck, "so make yourself at home."

The family of ducks made themselves comfortable, but life was not so easy for the ugly duckling. The other animals teased him, and pushed him, and nipped him with their beaks. Even the old turkey, who thought himself to be an emperor, puffed himself up and declared to anyone who would listen that the duckling was altogether too big. He shouted about it for so long that he turned quite red in the face. The poor duckling was attacked from every direction and so had no idea which way to turn. His life was miserable.

And things got worse with every day that passed. His own brothers and sisters turned against him, spitefully whispering loud enough for him to hear, "Oh he's so ugly, I wish the cat would get him." Even his own mother was so ashamed of him that she wished he had never been born. The ducks pecked him, the chickens scratched him and the girl who fed them all kicked him.

Finally the duckling could take no more and he ran away, scaring all the animals in the hedge as he flew past. "They hate me because I'm so ugly," thought the duckling, and he flew on and on until he could fly no more. He landed in a large water meadow where the wild ducks lived.

The ducks looked at their new visitor and said, "What sort of duck are you? You're very ugly, but that doesn't bother us, as long as you don't want to marry any of our family."

That poor duckling. All he wanted was somewhere to rest his weary head without being pecked or kicked. He'd never even thought of marriage, which sounded like one more problem he could do without.

Two days later a couple of goslings appeared in the meadow. They were quite cheeky but friendly enough. "Hello ugly!" they called. "Fancy joining us as we go on an adventure? We know where there are some wild ducks where even someone as ugly as you might find a wife."

As the goslings were the closest thing he had to friends he agreed to join them. As they took off a loud "Pop, pop!" sounded in the air and the two goslings fell down dead. At the noise flocks of wild geese rose from the reeds on the meadow, and the pop, pop sound came from everywhere. Huntsmen had hidden themselves all around and the smoke from their guns hung over the reeds like a thick cloud. The noise seemed to go on forever.

The duckling crouched low on the ground and covered his head with a wing. When he peeped out he was looking straight at an enormous hunting dog. The dog was so close that the duckling could see the dog's sharp teeth and feel its hot damp breath.

The dog stared at the duckling for a couple of seconds before he turned about and splashed off across the meadow.

"I'm so ugly," thought the duckling, "that even a dog won't eat me."

And he covered his head with his wing again and listened to the sound of the guns and the barking dogs. After several hours all was quiet. The duckling got up and ran and ran across the meadows until a storm blew up and he could run no more.

By the evening he had struggled to a small cottage that was so ramshackle it looked like it might fall down at any minute. The duckling flopped down beside the cottage and noticed that there was a small gap in the door. He slipped through the gap and snuggled down in a corner for the night.

An old woman lived in the cottage with her pet cat and a hen. The woman treated the cat like her son, but it was quite a fearsome creature. The hen had very short legs, and was called "Chickie short legs" for this reason. But she laid good eggs and for this reason the old woman loved her, too.

In the morning the cat discovered their new visitor and began to purr loudly, which set the hen off who clucked just as noisily.

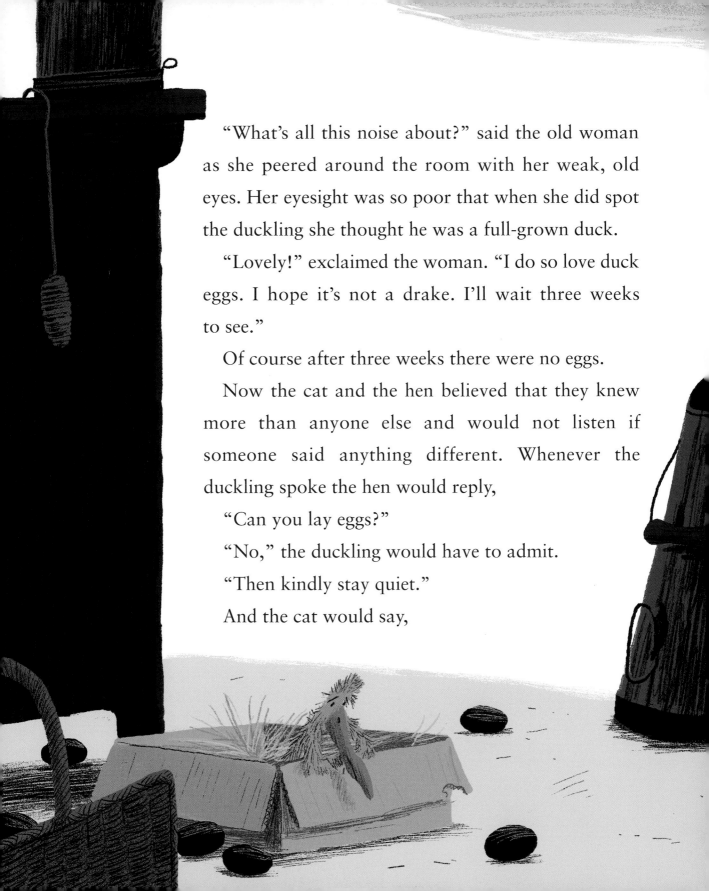

"What's all this noise about?" said the old woman as she peered around the room with her weak, old eyes. Her eyesight was so poor that when she did spot the duckling she thought he was a full-grown duck.

"Lovely!" exclaimed the woman. "I do so love duck eggs. I hope it's not a drake. I'll wait three weeks to see."

Of course after three weeks there were no eggs.

Now the cat and the hen believed that they knew more than anyone else and would not listen if someone said anything different. Whenever the duckling spoke the hen would reply,

"Can you lay eggs?"

"No," the duckling would have to admit.

"Then kindly stay quiet."

And the cat would say,

"Can you purr, or arch your back?"

"No," the duckling would reply.

"Then you have no right to talk when your betters are speaking."

And the duckling sat in the corner feeling very low.

He could feel the fresh breeze blowing through the gap in the door and longed for the feel of the sun and the water. He told the hen how he felt.

"What an absurd idea!" said the hen. "Your problem is you have nothing to do, so your mind wanders. If you could purr or lay eggs you wouldn't think about such things."

"But swimming is so much fun," said the duckling, "the water is so cool and refreshing when you dive into it."

"What nonsense!" said the hen. "Ask the cat what he thinks about diving about in water. He's by far the cleverest animal I know, so I'll not give my opinion. In fact ask our mistress, you'll not meet a more intelligent person. Do you think she enjoys swimming or diving around the place?"

"No, you don't understand me," said the duck.

"We don't understand you?" cried the hen. "Do you think that you're more intelligent than the cat, or our mistress? You don't realise quite how lucky you are. Here you are in fine surroundings where you could learn from educated people, but instead you chatter on all day. I advise you to learn how to purr and lay eggs as soon as possible."

"I think I had better leave," said the duckling.

"Yes, I think it would be for the best!" snapped the hen.

So the duckling left the cottage and found a pond where he could swim and dive. It was an unattractive little pond really and other ducks avoided it, so the duckling was left to his own devices.

Autumn came and the leaves on the trees turned orange and gold. Autumn passed and winter came and the falling leaves were replaced by snow and hail. The clouds hung low in the sky and the only noise to be heard was the crowing of the rooks. It was a cold and desolate place.

Then one evening, just as the sun was setting, a large flock of beautiful birds flew overhead. The

duckling had never seen anything like them before. They were swans with dazzling white feathers and graceful long necks. With a low cry they disappeared into the distance, off to warmer lands to avoid the winter. As they flew further and further away the ugly duckling felt a bit odd and uttered a cry that was so odd he surprised himself.

When at last they were out of sight he dived under the water and rose again, beside himself with excitement. He didn't know what those magnificent birds were called or where they were going, but he knew he would never forget them. How he wished he was like them.

The days grew colder and colder and the duckling had to swim about on the pond to stop it from freezing over. But every night the space left for the duckling to swim in grew smaller and smaller. Eventually the ice closed in completely and the duckling found himself stuck fast.

The next morning a passing peasant spotted the unfortunate duckling. Using his shoe he broke the ice and took the bird back to his wife. But their children were so excited that the duckling took fright at all the noise and started up in terror. He flapped straight into a milk pan and splashed milk everywhere. The woman

clapped her hands which frightened the bird even more. He flew into a butter-churn and then into a flour tub. What a mess! The woman screamed and tried to hit him with some tongs, the children shouted and jumped about but the bird managed to squeeze out of the door and slipped into the rushes.

It would be too sad to tell you of the terrible time the duckling had that winter, but eventually he felt the warm sun shining and realised that spring had crept into the air.

He tried his wings, which beat strongly against his sides and soon he was flying into the blue sky. He looked down and spotted a large garden. The trees were in blossom and the willows trailed their long fingers in a deep, slow river. It looked beautiful. And what's more, there on the river floated three of those beautiful birds the duckling had seen that winter's day. The sight made him feel strangely sad.

"If I go to those beautiful birds they will kill me because I am so ugly," he thought. "But, better to be killed by them than be pecked by ducks or scratched by hens, or kicked by girls who feed the birds."

So he went down to the water and swam towards the swans.

"Kill me," said the bird and bent his head down to the water to await his fate. But what do you think he saw peering back at him from the river?

The reflection of a swan – his own reflection! He was no longer a big, ugly duckling, in fact he never had been. He had come from a swan's egg and had been a baby swan, not a baby duck.

He was overcome with joy, happiness made all the sweeter for having suffered so much in the past. The other swans surrounded him and stroked his neck in greeting.

Some children then came into the garden to feed the swans with some cake and bread.

"See!" cried one, "there is a new one!" The children ran to their mother and father shouting:

"A new swan, a new swan, another one has come."

As they fed the swans they claimed that the new swan was the most beautiful one of all, and the other swans agreed with the children.

The swan was embarrassed by all this attention, for he had never been so loved in his entire life. The sun was warm on his back as he stretched out his graceful neck and fluffed up his brilliant white feathers. And from the depths of his heart he cried out "I never dreamed of such happiness while I was an ugly duckling!"

THE PRINCESS AND THE PEA

Once upon a time there was a prince and, as princes do, he wanted to marry a princess. But real princesses were hard to find and the prince travelled all over the world looking for one. Whenever he found a princess, there was always something about them that was not quite right, so he always returned home a disappointed young man.

One evening there was a terrible storm with loud claps of thunder, bright flashes of lightning and the heaviest rain you have ever seen. In the middle of the storm there was a loud knock at the palace gates which the old king himself went to answer.

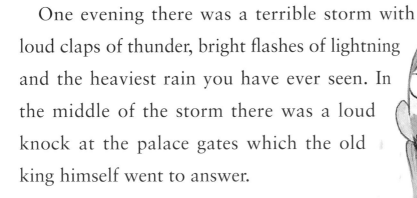

Huddled by the gate was a young woman. Her clothes were so wet that the water ran right down her body, down into her shoes and out through the toes. The old king brought her into the palace to shelter for the night.

"I'm a princess," said the girl.

"Well, we'll see about that," thought the queen. And off she went to fetch every mattress in the palace and put it on the princess' bed. And underneath the bottom mattress the queen placed a pea.

The next morning the queen asked the princess how she had slept.

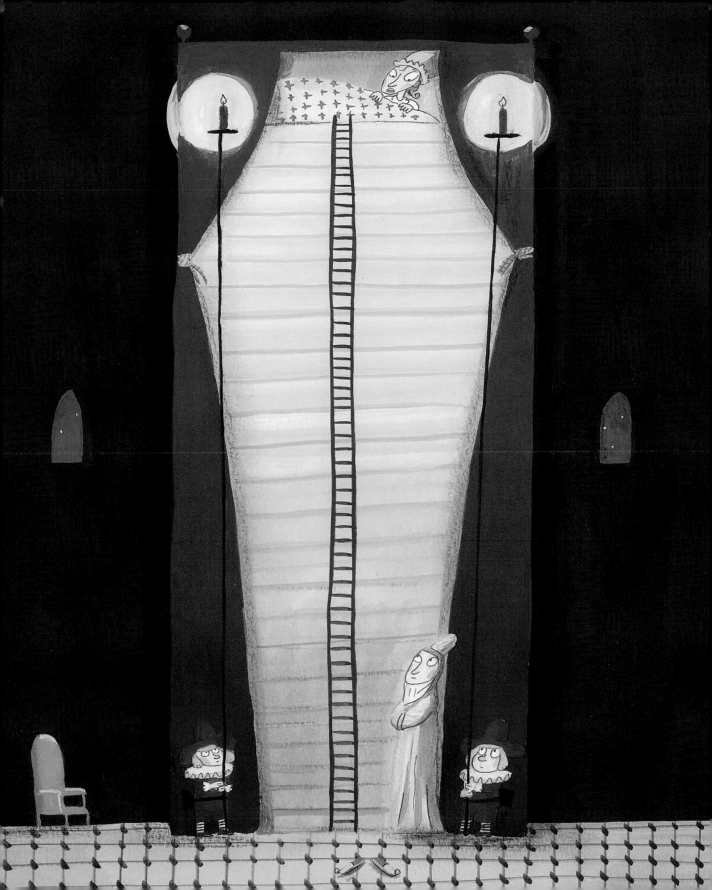

"Oh, very badly!" she replied. "I've barely had a wink of sleep all night. There was something so hard in that bed that I'm black and blue all over."

Now they knew that she must be a princess because she had felt a pea underneath all those mattresses. No one but a real princess could be as sensitive as that.

So the prince took the princess as his wife, for he knew he had finally found the girl of his dreams. The pea was put into a museum and you can still see it to this day, which is all the proof you need that this is a true story.

THE THREE LITTLE PIGS

There was once a poor old pig whose three children were eating her out of house and home. They were not bad little pigs, they were just growing and had big healthy appetites the way young pigs do.

"My dear children," said the old sow, "our house is not a big house and the time has come for you to find your own way in the world. My legs are weak, my eyes are tired and I cannot look after you any more."

The little pigs realised that their mother told the truth and, with heavy hearts, they left to build their own homes.

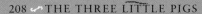

The first pig found a bundle of straw and quickly built himself a house. Then off he went hunting for apples.

The second pig collected himself some sticks and took a little longer to build himself a better house than his brother.

The third pig didn't like the look of his brothers' homes. Instead he got himself some bricks and built himself a fine, strong house with a stout front door and a sturdy little chimney.

Presently a hungry wolf passed by. He saw the first little pig's house and said:

"Little pig, little pig, let me come in."

"Not by the hair on my chinny-chin-chin," replied the little pig.

"Well, then I'll huff and I'll puff and I'll blow your house down!" said the wolf.

And he huffed and he puffed and he blew the little straw house away. Seeing his house disappearing around him the little pig scampered off as fast as his trotters could carry him to his brother's house.

No sooner had the little pig arrived at the house made of sticks, than the wolf appeared. The second pig pulled his brother inside and slammed the door shut.

The wolf padded up to the door and said:

"Little pig, little pig, let me come in."

"Not by the hair on my chinny-chin-chin," replied the second little pig.

"Well, then I'll huff and I'll puff and I'll blow your house down!" said the wolf.

And he huffed and he puffed and he blew the little stick house away.

Seeing the stick house disappearing around them, the two little pigs ran as fast as their little trotters could carry them to their brother's house.

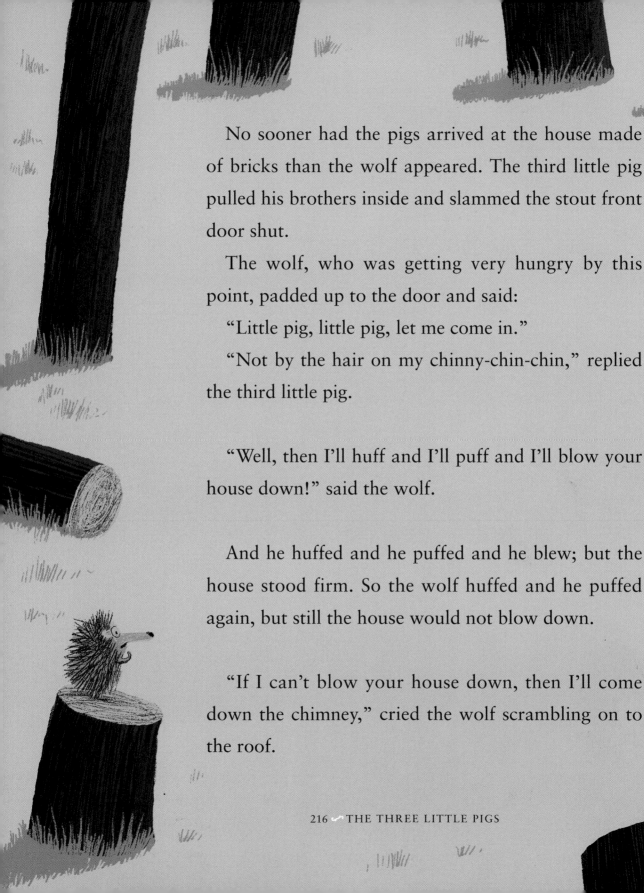

No sooner had the pigs arrived at the house made of bricks than the wolf appeared. The third little pig pulled his brothers inside and slammed the stout front door shut.

The wolf, who was getting very hungry by this point, padded up to the door and said:

"Little pig, little pig, let me come in."

"Not by the hair on my chinny-chin-chin," replied the third little pig.

"Well, then I'll huff and I'll puff and I'll blow your house down!" said the wolf.

And he huffed and he puffed and he blew; but the house stood firm. So the wolf huffed and he puffed again, but still the house would not blow down.

"If I can't blow your house down, then I'll come down the chimney," cried the wolf scrambling on to the roof.

The first two little pigs were so scared they started
to cry, but the third little pig told them not to worry.

As the wolf squeezed his way down the chimney,
the third little pig calmly lit a huge fire in the grate.
When the wolf finally popped out of the bottom of
the chimney he dropped, bump, straight into the hot
flames. He shot back up the chimney with a wild howl
and ran off into the distance, never to be seen again.

The third little pig invited his brothers to stay, for his house was big enough for all of them. And this included their mother, of course, who was overjoyed to be reunited with her beloved children. And they all lived happily ever after.

There once was a very rich man with more money and carriages than you could possibly imagine. However, the man had a bright blue beard, so although he was the richest man in the land, he was also the ugliest. Despite his blue beard the man had been married seven times, but no one knew what become of his wives for each of them had disappeared.

Now the man had fallen in love with his neighbour's two daughters, and wished to marry one of them. Neither girl wanted to marry a man with a blue beard, of course, and they were also worried about the fate of the missing wives.

Blue Beard would not be put off though, and arranged a party for all of the people of the village in the garden of his splendid house. Blue Beard was the perfect host and everyone had a fabulous time. Seeing Blue Beard's generosity and kindness, the youngest daughter's heart began to melt and she fell in love with him. As soon as they returned to the village they were married.

About a month later Blue Beard informed his wife that he had to go away for about six weeks on business. While he was gone, he told her, she should invite some friends round to keep herself amused.

"Here are the keys to every door in the house," he said. "This one opens my money boxes, this one all my chambers, this one my wardrobes and this one my cupboards. And this little one opens the small door at the end of the gallery on the ground floor. You are

allowed to open any door you please, except for the door unlocked by this small key. I forbid you to go in there; if I find you have I will be furious."

She promised to do as he had said and Blue Beard got into his carriage and left.

Blue Beard's wife wasted no time in inviting her sister to stay and her friends to visit the magnificent house. They were only too keen to come as they were all curious to see inside the house of the man with the blue beard.

They ran through the rooms and opened every door and gazed in wonder at the fine clothes and beautiful ornaments. They gasped at the huge tapestries and gilded furniture and were amazed by the fine paintings and ornate mirrors. However, all the while, the wife was impatient to see what lay behind the small door at the end of the gallery on the ground floor.

Seeing that her friends were so engrossed with looking at Blue Beard's fine possessions, she sneaked away to go to the door.

She hurried down the stairs and along the gallery and was soon standing in front of the forbidden door. She took the little key and unlocked it.

At first she couldn't see anything because the windows were covered by shutters. Slowly, her eyes got used to the gloom; but what she saw chilled her to the bone. There on a blood soaked floor were the bodies of Blue Beard's seven other wives! She slammed the door shut, locked it and raced upstairs.

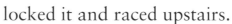

The wife was gasping with fright and hid herself away in her chambers. To make matters worse she noticed that the key to the small door was covered in blood! She tried to wipe the blood off, but the stain wouldn't shift. She tried washing it and scraping at it, but as soon as she had cleaned the stain from one side of the key, it reappeared on the other.

That very evening Blue Beard returned home. He explained that he had heard on the way that he was not needed at the meeting, and his wife tried her best to look overjoyed at his unexpected return.

The next morning Blue Beard asked for his keys. His wife returned them with a trembling hand.

"Why is the little key not here?" he asked.

"I must have left it on the table," she lied.

"Well bring it to me," replied Blue Beard.

After several false trips backwards and forwards the wife was forced to bring Blue Beard the key.

"Why is there blood on the key?" asked Blue Beard.

"I-I-I don't know," stammered his wife in return.

"You don't know!" cried Blue Beard. "Well I know! You have been in the room which I forbade you to enter. Well, my dear, the time has come for you to join those other ladies."

The wife threw herself upon the ground and begged his pardon. Her pleading would have melted the hardest of hearts, but Blue Beard was unmoved.

"No my dear, you must die and die now."

"If I am to be killed," replied the wife, "then allow me some time to say my prayers first."

"Very well," said Blue Beard, "you have quarter of an hour, but no longer."

As soon as Blue Beard left, the wife called for her sister. "Sister, sister, go to the top of the tower and look out for our brothers. They had promised to be here today. If you see them signal for them to hurry."

The sister climbed the tower and scanned the horizon. Every so often the poor wife would call out:

"Sister, sister, do you see them?"

And the sister would reply:

"I see nothing but the sun and the grass."

In the meantime Blue Beard had fetched a large sword and shouted:

"Come down wife, your time is up!"

"One moment longer," pleaded the wife. Then, as softly as she could, she asked her sister if she could see anyone.

But the sister replied:

"I see nothing but the sun and the grass."

"Wife, come down quickly," shouted Blue Beard, "or I shall come up!"

"I'm coming," sighed the wife. Then she asked her sister once again:

"Sister, sister, do you see anyone?"

"I see a great cloud of dust coming from the right," she replied.

"Is it our brothers?" asked the wife.

"Alas no," replied the sister. "It is but a flock of sheep."

"Will you not come down?" cried Blue Beard.

"I'm coming," replied the wife. And one last time she asked her sister:

"Sister, sister, do you see anyone?"

And her sister replied:

"I see two horsemen, but they are a long way away."

"Oh it is our brothers!" cried the wife. "I shall make a sign for them to hurry."

Then Blue Beard shouted a final time, a shout so loud the very timbers of the house shook.

Seeing that there was no way of delaying any further, the wife went downstairs. She pleaded and wept but to no avail.

"Spare me your tears, wife, it is time to die." And Blue Beard grabbed hold of her hair in one hand and raised his sword in the other ready to strike. "Prepare to meet thy maker."

At that precise moment two men burst through the front door. It was the wife's brothers. Seeing their sister in such danger, they drew their swords and rushed at Blue Beard, who promptly dropped the woman and turned to run. But the brothers were more nimble and caught Blue Beard and ran him through with their swords.

Now Blue Beard had no heirs, so his wife inherited all his belongings. With the evil murderer gone, his fine houses became welcoming places which people from near and far were happy to visit. As for the wife, she met a fine young gentleman with whom she fell in love and soon forgot the time she spent with the terrible Blue Beard.